A Visit with Great-Grandma

Sharon Hart Addy

pictures by Lydia Halverson

ALBERT WHITMAN & COMPANY, NILES, ILLINOIS

To my family, my Czechoslovakian friends,
especially Barb Blaskowski and Camilla Berg,
the Wisconsin Slovak Historical Society,
and all the others who helped make this book
possible. S.H.A.

To Mom, for her encouragement. L.H.

Text © 1989 by Sharon Hart Addy
Illustrations © 1989 by Lydia Halverson

Published in 1989 by Albert Whitman & Company,
5747 W. Howard St., Niles, Illinois 60648
Published simultaneously in Canada by
General Publishing, Limited, Toronto

Library of Congress Cataloging-in-Publication Data

Addy, Sharon.
    A visit with great-grandma / Sharon Hart Addy;
illustrated by Lydia Halverson.
        p.   cm.
    Summary: Even though Great-grandma speaks very little
English and Baruška does not speak Czech, they enjoy
a very special afternoon together while baking and
looking at old photographs. ISBN 0-8075-8497-5
    [1. Great-grandmothers—Fiction.
2. Czech Americans—Fiction.]
I. Halverson, Lydia, ill. II. Title.   88-20867
PZ7.A257Vi 1989   CIP
[E]—dc19   AC

STRAWBERRY KOLACH

2 packages dry yeast
1/4 cup warm water
6 cups flour
1/2 cup sugar
1 teaspoon salt
1 cup butter

3 egg yolks, beaten
1 teaspoon vanilla
1 can (12 oz.) evaporated milk
melted butter
strawberry jam

Soften the yeast in warm water. Combine flour, sugar, and salt in a large bowl. Cut in the butter. Mix in egg yolks, vanilla, milk, and yeast. Then shape the dough into a ball. Place in a greased bowl. Cover and let rise for about 2½ hours or until double in size. Roll out to a circle about 18-20 inches in diameter. Cut into quarters and spread generously with strawberry jam. Roll up each quarter and place on an ungreased jelly roll pan. Let rise until double in size. Brush with melted butter and bake at 350 degrees F. for 40 minutes.

The recipe given here is just one way to make kolach. There are many other ways to prepare this traditional Czechoslovakian dessert.

When Grandma and I go to visit Great-grandma, Great-grandma gives me a hug. "Baruška!" she says. *Baruška* means "little Barbara" in Slovak. Her name is Barborka, or Barbara—I'm named for her.

Great-grandma doesn't know much English. She's from Czechoslovakia and speaks Slovak.

"I came to help you, Starenka," I tell her. *Starenka* means grandmother.

Great-grandma's apartment is full of wonderful things. In the living room she has eggs with beautiful designs on them. She and her friends painted them when she lived in the old country.

Grandma and Great-grandma talk in Slovak at the kitchen table. Their voices make a soft, whispery sound. Great-grandma gives Grandma a shopping list.

When Grandma leaves for the store, Great-grandma says, "Make kolach. Strawberry?" She smiles so big the lines in her face get deeper, and her cheeks puff to her eyes. She knows strawberry is my favorite. Momma likes nut, and Daddy likes poppy seed.

Great-grandma hands me an apron. She wraps the strings around to the front, and I tie them.

Then she measures warm water into a bowl and opens a package of yeast with her crooked fingers.

"Can I do that?" I ask. I point to her fingers and then to me, so she knows what I mean.

Great-grandma nods yes.

She hands me a wooden spoon. I stir too fast. The water jumps up the side of the bowl. Great-grandma lays her soft hand on my arm. "Baruška," she says and frowns. I stir more slowly.

Together we measure flour and sugar into a bigger bowl with a
bright design on it. She mixes in the butter and adds egg yolks,
canned milk, and the yeast I mixed with water.

Great-grandmother stirs slower and slower. Then she stops. "I no
can do," she says. "I old."

"Let me try, Starenka," I say, and I take the spoon. The dough is heavy and hard to push. I can hardly move it.

"I can't do it, and I'm not old!" I say. I make an awful face.

Great-grandma laughs.

"Mixer," she says and points to it.

The mixer whirs, and a puff of white flies from the bowl.

When the dough is mixed, Starenka covers it so it will rise.

Then we stack the dishes in the sink and go into the living room.

Great-grandma has pictures everywhere. She has pictures of my grandma and my momma and uncles when they were little. She has yellowy pictures of her momma and poppa. And she has pictures of her brothers and sisters and where they live in the old country.

Great-grandma picks up a picture of a man with a beard.
"Poppa," she says. She points to herself. She means he was her
poppa. "Poppa like kolach," she says and smiles. "Big." She pats
her arm so I know she means he was strong.

Once she told me he grew vegetables and had a cow. "Was he a farmer?" I ask.

She shakes her head no. Then she moves her head from side to side to show she's trying to remember a word.

"Horses," she says. "Topanky." She points to her feet.
"Shoes?" I guess. "Your Poppa made shoes for horses?"
Great-grandma nods her head yes.

POPELKA
Byla jedna vdova, měla tři
dcery: dvě vlastní a jednu nevlastní.
Těm svým dcerám přála, krásně je
strojila, všechno jim dávala, nač jen si
vzpomněly. Té nevlastní nepřála, ani najíst
jí nedávala, jen ji do práce honila. Od úsvitu
musila pracovat, za to nesměla
za jedním stolem sedat,
kytlici a lůžko
celý den

I want to look at Great-grandma's storybook. I go to the cabinet and point to it.

Great-grandma smiles and pats the couch next to her.

The writing in the book is different. The letters are squiggly, and there are lots of dots. The pictures are beautiful.

At one picture Great-grandma taps the book. "Cinderella," she says. "I like." She smooths my hair and says something in that soft other language.

I think she's imagining it's long ago. Maybe her mother read to her when she was little. When she looks at me, I just smile. Great-grandma smiles back, and we have a secret.

We sit and look at the book a long time. Great-grandma's wooden wind-up clock goes tic-tic, tic-tic, over and over, and then it chimes. We go to the kitchen. I watch as Great-grandma flattens the dough and cuts it into four pieces. She spreads strawberry jam over one piece for me. She spreads nut and poppy-seed fillings over the other three. Then she rolls them up, puts them on cookie sheets, and covers them with a towel.

We do the dishes while we wait for the kolach to rise again.

When it is in the oven, we go to the dining room. Great-grandma has two Czechoslovakian dolls, a boy and a girl dressed for dancing. I want to touch them, but they are very special. Great-grandma sees me looking but not touching, and she smiles. I'm glad I make her happy.

She picks them up and gives them to me. I sit on the floor and pretend they are dancing while she hums a tune.

When she stops humming, she motions for me to put the dolls back. She takes the lace cloth off the table and gets out her flower plates. We set the table together. The kolach is filling the house with warm, sweet smells.

The phone rings while we are peeking in the oven. Great-grandma answers. Then she says, "I no talk good English." She gives the phone to me.

I listen. "He wants to know if you need windows." I point to the windows.

Great-grandma makes a funny, frowning face. She shakes her head no.

"She has windows," I tell the man and say goodbye.

"Why didn't you talk to him?" I ask Great-grandma. "You talk to me."

"Too fast English," she says. "I no understand they. They no understand me."

"I understand you," I say.

"You listen ears, eyes, heart."

I point to my ears, eyes, and heart the way Great-grandma did. She smiles and nods.

The timer on the stove dings. "Ah," Great-grandma says, "kolach ready."

We sprinkle the kolach with powdered sugar and set it on the
dining-room table.

Great-grandma puts the first piece on my plate. I didn't ask for it.
Great-grandma listened with her heart.